Bingo Lingo

Supporting language development through songs and rhymes

Helen MacGregor

With additional material by Kaye Umansky

Literacy consultant: Lynn Mills
With illustrations by Michael Evans

A & C Black • London

Contents

Introduction

First published 1999
Reprinted 2000, 2002
A & C Black Publishers Ltd
37 Soho Square
London W1D 3QZ
www.acblack.com

ISBN 0 7136 5075 3

Author: Helen MacGregor
Additional songs and rhymes: Kaye Umansky
Literacy consultant: Lynn Mills
Editor: Ana Sanderson
Designer: Dorothy Moir
Illustrator: Michael Evans
Cover artist: Alex Ayliffe
A & C Black uses paper produced with elemental chlorine-free pulp, harvested from managed sustainable forests.
Printed in Great Britain by St Edmundsbury Press, Bury St Edmunds, Suffolk.

Text © Helen MacGregor 1999
Illustrations © Michael Evans 1999
Cover artwork © Alex Ayliffe 1999

From infancy, children gain great pleasure from the songs, rhymes and rhythms which help them to remember words and develop good listening skills. **Bingo Lingo** is a resource full of material that will capture children's imaginations. It was written and compiled for that exciting stage in a child's development when (s)he begins to develop sound (phonological) awareness and experience the spoken language system upon which the development of literacy relies.

Playing with sounds

These activities encourage children to explore vocal sounds: remembering and copying; inventing their own; and investigating patterns of sound through songs and chants. There are many opportunities for links with writing; e.g. the animal sounds suggested by the children for *Old MacGregor had a zoo* can be made into a frieze by the children or scribed by the teacher as appropriate.

Rhyme

The musical games and songs in this section build a child's memory for the pitch, tone and intensity of language as well as providing a fun way of improving phonological awareness. In this section, the focus is on rhyme, through which children learn to categorise words by sound, increasing their potential to read and write. Experience of rhyming words later leads to comparisons of different spellings of the same sounds. The songs here give children experience of rhymes and also opportunities for predicting and making their own rhyming phrases. Rhyme also draws attention to the two very important language units: onset and rime.

Onset and rime

There are three levels of phonological awareness: syllables; onset and rime; and phonemes. Children need to be able to break words into syllables before they can break them into phonemes, and they naturally find it much simpler to break up words into 'onsets' and 'rimes' than into single phonemes (*b-est* rather than *b-e-s-t;*

w-in/d-ow rather than *w-i-n-d-o-w*). The songs here are based on changing onsets which reinforce the child's understanding of these two elements, as in *Spooky song's h-oo, b-oo, sh-oo, wh-oo.*

Alphabet and letters; word endings; grammar

The last three sections of the book provide musical activities with more specific teaching points, including the use of 'magic e', word endings, adjectives and opposites. Many of these can be used with children whose literacy skills are more advanced and they provide more opportunities for reading and writing.

Teacher's notes

The following symbols are used in the teacher's notes:

 This indicates a basic description of the song.

 This gives more literacy development with questions, investigations or extensions.

 This indicates a musical activity.

A summary of the literacy focus of each song, rhyme or rap can be found in the bottom right hand corner of the page, together with the section heading.

The first notes of each tune are indicated in the bottom left hand corner of the page. If any tune is unknown to you, you will find it written out at the back of the book, together with the new words. If you don't read music, find someone who does to teach the songs to you. If you know a different version of a tune from the one we have given, do use it as the new words will still fit.

The songs and chants in **Bingo Lingo** are simple to incorporate into daily classroom routines, enabling a multi-sensory approach to literacy work necessary to compensate for weaknesses, while building on strengths. Let the essential elements of active participation and fun enhance the learning of your children!

Helen MacGregor and Lynn Mills

All the songs and rhymes in this collection were written by Helen MacGregor, except for the following by Kaye Umansky:
12 Captain of the aeroplane, 13 Whatever the weather, 17 No room, 18 A plate of potatoes, 19 Little red jeep, 27 Alphabet's tea, 34 The wishing well, 35 Quick, duck, quack, 36 Huff, puff, and *37 Party time;*
© Kaye Umansky 1999.
3 Some names is an adaptation of the song *Some sounds are short* by Sue Nicholls, in *Bobby Shaftoe, clap your hands,* published by A & C Black.

The author and publishers would like to thank the following people for their generous help during the preparation of this book: Paul Gregory, Marion Lang, Alasdair MacGregor, Audrey Mason, Sue Nicholls, Linda Read, Sheena Roberts and Jane Sebba.

1 Hello around the world

Tune: *If you're happy and you know it*

Solo:	**All (chant):**
When you want to say *hello* around the world,	Hello!
When you want to say *hello* around the world,	Hello!
When you want to say *hello*,	
Sing this song and you will know	
How to greet your friends from all around the world.	Hello!
When you greet your friends in *French* you say *bonjour.*	Bonjour!
When you greet your friends in *French* you say *bonjour.*	Bonjour!
When you want to say *hello*,	
Sing this song and you will know	
When you greet your friends in *French* you say *bonjour.*	Bonjour!
When you greet your friends in *Hindi* you say *namusti* ...	Namusti!
When you greet your friends in *Italian* you say *ciao* ...	Ciao!

☆ This song is a useful starting point for collecting and comparing greetings from different cultures. Continue adding more verses using languages relevant to the children. Here are some additional examples together with pronunciation guides: *Swahili: jambo (**jam**boh); Spanish: hola (**oh**la); Mandarin: hi (high); Yoruba: bawoni (ba**woh**nee).*

C   C   F   F   F   F F F E   F   G

If you want to say *hel-lo* a-round the world   **greetings in other languages**

2 Jamaquacks

Circle game

Jamaquack, jamaquack, jamaquack jive,
Jamaquacks sing when the clock strikes five.
One, two, three, four, five.

> *Sam:* zeeeeeeee
> *All:* zeeeeeee

Jamaquack, jamaquack, jamaquack jive,
Jamaquacks sing when the clock strikes five.
One, two, three, four, five.

> *Kate:* lee li lee li lo
> *All:* lee li lee li lo ...

☆ This circle game encourages children to invent, memorise and copy vocal sounds. Jamaquacks are imaginary creatures who speak a made-up language. The children sit in a circle and pass a toy microphone around as they say the chant together. Whoever is holding the microphone on number five makes up a jamaquack word or phrase. The rest of the children copy it and the game continues.

**playing with sounds
inventing and copying**

3 Some names

Tune: Pease pudding hot

Some names are short,
Some names are long.
Please tell us your name
After this song.

D   D   E   F♯
Some names are short

☆ Explore children's names. Find similarities, e.g. those which begin with the same letter or sound. If you wish, explore the number of syllables in names.

**playing with sounds
exploring names**

4 Old MacGregor had a zoo

Old MacDonald had a farm – adapted

Old MacGregor had a zoo, ee i ee i o.
And in that zoo she had some *snakes*, ee i ee i o.
   With a *ssss ssss* here and a *ssss ssss* there,
   Here a *ssss*, there a *ssss*, everywhere a *ssss ssss*,
Old MacGregor had a zoo, ee i ee i o.

... *hippos* ... *grum grum* ...

... *parrots* ... *hello hello* ...

☆ Explore letter sounds through to whole words in this version of the old favourite. The children make up new verses by choosing their own selection of animals and their sounds.

🚀 Make a frieze illustrating the animals and the sounds the children have suggested. Use this to investigate letter sounds and digraphs, made-up words, and whole words.

G G G D E E D
Old Mac-Gre-gor had a zoo

playing with sounds
developing awareness of sounds

5 Mashed potato

Chant

Scrub-a-dub, scrub-a-dub,
Chip-chop, chip-chop,
Hubble-bubble, hubble-bubble,
Mish-mash, mish-mash,
Mmmmmmmmmmm.

 Perform this chant with rhythmic hand actions for each line.

 Perform it as a round.

**playing with sounds
patterns of sounds**

6 Chatterbox

Tune: Pat-a-cake

Chatterbox, chatterbox chats all day,
Chatterbox can't hear what I want to say.
Chattering, nattering, yackety-yack,
Chatterbox, chatterbox, let me talk back!

Chanted word patterns:
1 Yac - ke - ty, yac - ke - ty, yac - ke - ty yack (x4)
2 Clac - ke - ty clack, clac - ke - ty clack (x4)
3 Jab - ber and blab - ber, jab - ber and blab-ber (x4)

☆ Alternate singing the verse with chanting each word pattern four times.

🚀 Divide the children into three groups to chant the word patterns at the same time, to make a chattering effect.

🚀 Suggest more word patterns, e.g. *chatter, natter; mumble, grumble.*

C E G C E G G F F
Chat-ter-box, chat-ter-box chats all day

**playing with sounds
patterns of sounds**

7 My machine

Tune: The wheels on the bus

Today I made a fine machine,
Fine machine, fine machine,
Today I made a fine machine,
See it work.

The cogs have teeth on my machine,
My machine, my machine,
The cogs have teeth on my machine,
Can you hear?
    Chant: *Trick-track, trick-track, trick-track, trick-track (x4)*

The wheels spin round on my machine,
My machine, my machine,
The wheels spin round on my machine,
Can you hear?
    Chant: *Zoop,   zoop,   zoop,   zoop (x4)*

Springs coil and stretch on my machine ...
    Chant: *Boing,   shhhhhhhhhhh (x4)*

The levers move on my machine ...
    Chant: *Um-chicky-um-pah,   um-chicky-um-pah (x4)*

The whistle blows on my machine ...
> **Chant:** *Beebeeeeeeeeeep,   beebeeeeeeeeeep* (x4)

Today I made a fine machine,
Fine machine, fine machine,
Today I made a fine machine,
Can you hear?
> **Chant:** *Trick-track, trick-track, trick-track, trick-track ...*
> *Zoop,   zoop,   zoop,   zoop ...*
> *Boing,   shhhhhhhhhhh ...*
> *Um-chicky-um-pah,   um-chicky-um-pah ...*
> *Beebeeeeeeeeeep,   beebeeeeeeeeeep ...*

☆ Teach this song one verse at a time, comparing the chanted sound effects at the end of each verse. Ask the children to contribute different ways of using their voices to say each sound, e.g. making voices swoop from low to high on *zoop*.

🚀 Divide the children into five groups to perform the chants one at a time. Can each group perform its chant independently? (You may need to tap a steady beat to prevent the performances from speeding up.)

🚀 Combine all five chants. Choose a conductor who signals to each group in turn to begin until all five are chanting simultaneously. The groups repeat their chants until the conductor signals either to stop or to perform an ending. (Perhaps the machine can get louder and louder until it blows up with a loud bang and a hiss!)

🚀 In small groups, individual children can invent new chanted sound effects, then together build a machine by combining the chants after the last verse. They may like to find ways of writing down their sounds in graphics or letters.

C F F F A C' A F
To-day I made a fine ma-chine

playing with sounds
patterns of sounds

8 Sleeping Beauty

Rap

The beginning (a very long time ago)

Let's tell the **sto**ry of	**Sleep**ing		**Beauty.**
Are you **rea**dy?	**Once** upon a		**time** –

– there was a **ba**by,	**Goo,**	*goo ga*	*goo,*
Her name was **Ro**sa;	**Goo,**	*goo ga*	*goo,*
The fairies **saw** her,	**Fly,**	*flee fly*	*flo,*
And made good **wish**es.	**Fly,**	*flee fly*	*flo,*
But then a **wick**ed witch	**Ha,**	*ha hee*	*ha,*
Waved her **ma**gic wand,	**Ha,**	*ha hee*	*ha,*
"Be careful, **Prin**cess,	**Whoa,**	*whoa whoa*	*whoa,*
Keep clear of **spin**ning wheels."	**Whoa,**	*whoa whoa*	*whoa.*

The middle (eighteen years later)

The princess **grew** up	**Grow,**	*grow grow*	*grow,*
From one to **eigh**teen,	**Grow,**	*grow grow*	*grow,*
And then di**sas**ter,	**No,**	*no no*	*no,*
She found a **spin**ning wheel.	**No,**	*no no*	*no,*
She pricked her **fin**ger,	**Ow,**	*ow ee*	*oh,*
Which made the **spell** work;	**Ow,**	*ow ee*	*oh,*
And she fell a**sleep**	**Sh,**	*sh sh*	*sh,*
For one hundred **years**.	**Sh,**	*sh sh*	*sh.*

The end (a century later)

	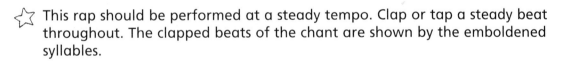			
A prince came **rid**ing	*Clop,*	*clop*	*clip*	*clop,*
Up to the **cas**tle;	*Clop,*	*clop*	*clip*	*clop,*
He started **chop**ping	*Chop,*	*chop*	*chip*	*chop,*
Through all the **bram**bles.	*Chop,*	*chop*	*chip*	*chop,*
Then he kissed **Ro**sa	*Kiss,*	*kiss*	*kiss*	*kiss,*
To break the **bad** spell.	*Kiss,*	*kiss*	*kiss*	*kiss,*
And they were **mar**ried	*Ding,*	*ding*	*dong*	*ding,*
To sounds of **wed**ding bells;	*Ding,*	*ding*	*dong*	*ding,*
And they **lived**	*Ding,*	*ding*	*dong*	*ding,*
Very **hap**pily	*Ding,*	*ding*	*dong*	*ding.*
Ever **af**ter!				

☆ This rap should be performed at a steady tempo. Clap or tap a steady beat throughout. The clapped beats of the chant are shown by the emboldened syllables.

🚀 On first hearing, encourage the children to join in with the sound patterns (given in italics). They can make up actions to go with them. Younger children will enjoy making the sounds and actions after you say each line, while older children will enjoy learning the whole rap.

🚀 Choose another story the children know well and ask them to re-tell it, sequencing short phrases which alternate with simple sound patterns, e.g. *Once upon a time, doo, doo bee doo, there was a little red hen, cluck, cluck cluck cluck ...* You can scribe for the whole class as a piece of shared writing or work with small groups.

playing with sounds
patterns of sounds; sequencing

9 Storm

Vocal sound picture

Hush   hush

Splish   splash   splish   splash

Rush   dash   rush   dash

Splish   splash   splish   splash

Slish   slosh   slish   slosh

Splish   splash   splish   splash

Bash   lash   bash   lash

Splish   splash   splish   splash

Crash   flash

Splish splash   splish splash

Bash   lash   bash   lash

Splish   splash   splish   splash

Slish   slosh   slish   slosh

Splish   splash   splish   splash

Rush   dash   rush   dash

Splish   splash   splish   splash

Hush   hush

Splish   splash   splish   splash

Wishhhhhhhhhhhhhhhhhhhhhhhhhhhhhhhhhhhh............

☆ This evocation of a storm in vocal sounds – a sound picture – begins quietly, gets louder, then quieter again. Teach it by asking the children to say just the *splish splash splish splash* lines at first. They should follow your increase and decrease in volume as you say the alternate lines. Gradually teach them all the words.

🚀 Perform the sound picture in two groups, alternating lines.

♪♪ Perform the sound picture with one group of children repeating *splish splash* throughout, (as an ostinato) while a second group says the whole poem.

🚀 The children can make other vocal sound pictures by choosing and repeating collections of sounds and words, e.g. *hweee, pop, ooeeeooo* ... for a sound picture of a fairground.

playing with sounds
patterns of sounds; –sh endings

10 Yoyo

Tune: Oranges and lemons

Once I had a yoyo,
But my yoyo wouldn't go go.
My friend Flo said, "No no!
That is not the way to yoyo.

You roll it to the top top,
And then you let it drop drop.
When it climbs the string,
You don't do a thing.

Then give a little flick flick,
Now you've nearly learnt the trick trick."
But when I tried to yoyo,
It still wouldn't go go.

☆ When the children know this song, ask them to explore the rhyming words. Notice how the rhyming scheme of the first verse differs from that of the other two.

♫ Add an accompaniment to the second verse by sliding a hard beater up and down the bars of a xylophone.

C' C' A C' A F
Once I had a yo-yo

rhyme
exploring rhyme

11 Grandma and the flea

Tune: A sailor went to sea

My Grandma found a flea, flea, flea,
A-swimming in her tea, tea, tea.
She took a spoon and fished it out,
And gave the flea to me, me, me.

I made the flea a bed, bed, bed,
To rest his little head, head, head.
But when I went to say, "Good night,"
Well, this is what he said, said, said:

"I do not want to nap, nap, nap,
I'm not a sleepy chap, chap, chap.
I'd rather dance all through the night,
And make my feet go tap, tap, tap."

He danced all through the night, night, night,
Until the morning light, light, light.
When I woke up he winked his eye,
And hopped off out of sight, sight, sight.

My Grandma, she got up, up, up,
And made some tea to sup, sup, sup.
The flea was doing loop the loops,
And fell into her cup, cup, cup.

My Grandma found a flea, flea, flea ...
It starts again you see, see, see.

This is a never-ending song which introduces different rhymes in each verse: *flea, tea, me; bed, head, said ...*

Investigate the spelling patterns of the rhyming words with older children, as well as the different rhyming patterns.

G   C' G   A   G   E   G G
My Grand-ma found a flea, flea, flea

rhyme
experiencing rhyme

12 Captain of the aeroplane

Tune: John Brown's body

I'm captain of the aeroplane and this is my salute,
I've got shiny, silver buttons on my special captain's suit.
I climb into my cockpit and I strap myself in tight,
And we're off! Enjoy the flight!

Chorus: Can you hear the engines roaring?
               Soon we'll all be up and soaring,
               In the sky we'll go exploring
               Inside my aeroplane.

We rattle down the runway and we really pick up speed,
Then we rise into the heavens which are very high indeed.
We fly around for hours and hours as high as high can be,
And we're back in time for tea.

Chorus: Can you hear the engines roaring ...

☆ Ask the children to perform actions with this song.

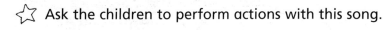

D   D   D   D C B,D G   A   B   B   B A G
I'm cap-tain of the ae-ro-plane and this is my sa-lute

rhyme
experiencing rhyme

13 Whatever the weather

Chant

Whether the weather is windy,
Whether the weather is grey,
We don't care whatever the weather,
We're going out to play!

Group 1:
Stiff breeze?
Warm sun?
Thick fog?
Hail storm?
Really hot?
Cold ice?
Hard rain?
Deep snow?

Group 2:
Yes, please!
That'll be fun!
Take the dog!
Wrap up warm!
So what!
That'll be nice!
Brolly again!
Cheerio!

Whether the weather is windy,
Whether the weather is grey,
We don't care whatever the weather,
We're going out to play!

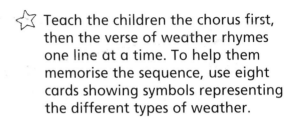

☆ Teach the children the chorus first, then the verse of weather rhymes one line at a time. To help them memorise the sequence, use eight cards showing symbols representing the different types of weather.

🚀 Divide the children into two groups to perform the verse as shown.

🚀 Point out to older children the use of question marks and exclamation marks.

♫ Ask the children to choose instrumental sounds to match each line of the verse, e.g. *stiff breeze* – shake maracas; *warm sun* – soft beater on a cymbal. Add these sounds to the verse, playing each sound with its matching line.

♫ Use the picture cards to cue the sequence of instrumental weather sounds as an interlude between speaking the verse and chorus, i.e. *chorus – instrumental sounds – verse – instrumental sounds – chorus.*

rhyme
experiencing rhyme; sequencing

14 Whoops!

Chant *(verse 1 – traditional)*

A peanut sat on the railway track,
His heart was all a-flutter,
Round the bend came number one,
Whoops! Peanut *butter!*

A strawberry sat on the railway track,
Her teeth were wobbling loose,
Round the bend came number two,
Whoops! Strawberry *mousse!*

A lemon sat on the railway track,
His eyes were on his belly,
Around the bend came number three,
Whoops! Lemon *jelly!*

An orange sat on the railway track,
Her face required a wash,
Round the bend came number four,
Whoops! Orange *squash!*

A tomato sat on the railway track,
His skin was red, of course,
Around the bend came number five,
Whoops! Tomato *sauce!*

14 Whoops! – photocopiable pictures

A potato sat on the railway track,
A smile was on his lips,
Around the bend came number six,
Whoops! Potato *chips!*

A biscuit sat on the railway track,
A-twiddling her thumbs,
Around the bend came number seven,
Whoops! Biscuit *crumbs!*

Some fruit and nuts sat on the track
Feeling rather sad,
A hungry traveller took them home,
Which wasn't quite so *bad!*
Or was it?

☆ Teach the first two verses to the children, then say
each following verse, omitting the final word (shown
in italics). Ask the children to supply the rhyming
word for each verse.

♫ Ask a small group of children to accompany the chant
with vocal train sounds, e.g. *choo choo choo choo* or
click clack click clack.

rhyme
predicting rhymes; number sequence

15 Hey, little playmate

Hush little baby – adapted (1st version)

Hey, little playmate, don't you cry,
I'm going to sing you a lullaby.

If that lullaby sounds too loud,
I'm going to buy you a little cloud.

If that little cloud starts to rain,
I'm going to buy you a railway train.

If that railway train leaves too soon,
I'm going to buy you a big balloon.

If that big balloon then goes pop,
I'm going to buy you a spinning top.

If that spinning top spins too fast,
The next gift I buy will be the last!

☆ Teach this new version of the traditional song to give experience of rhyming patterns.

D B B B C' B A A
Hey, lit-tle play-mate, don't you cry

rhyme
experiencing rhyme; sequencing

16 Hey, little playmate

Hush little baby – adapted (2nd version)

Hey, little playmate, don't say a thing,
I'm going to buy you a piece of *string*.

If that piece of string's too thick,
I'm going to buy you a baby *chick*.

If that baby chick won't cluck,
I'm going to buy you a plastic *duck*.

If that plastic duck won't float,
I'm going to buy you a sailing *boat*.

If that sailing boat won't go far,
I'm going to buy you a bright red *car*.

If that bright red car won't park,
I'm going to buy you a snapping *shark*.

If that snapping shark won't bite,
I'm going to buy you a big blue *kite*.

If that big blue kite won't fly,
I'm going to buy you an apple *pie*.

If that apple pie tastes funny,
I'm going to buy you a fluffy *bunny*.

If that fluffy bunny runs away,
That will be the last thing I buy *today*!

In this version of the song, the rhyming words are italicised. Omit them and ask the children to predict them.

With older children, investigate the spelling patterns of pairs of rhymes:
bite, kite – same spelling (rime); *pie, fly* – different spellings.

D B B B C' B A A A
Hey, lit-tle play-mate, don't say a thing

rhyme
predicting rhymes; sequencing

17 No room

Chant

I get in my bed at bedtime,
It's as crowded as can be.
    I sleep with a doll, I sleep with a troll,
There's hardly room for me!

I get in my bed at bedtime,
It's as crowded as can be.
    I'm into the habit of cuddling rabbit,
    I sleep with a doll, I sleep with a troll,
There's hardly room for me!

    ... I've got to have Ted, right here by my head ...

    ... My armadillo is under the pillow ...

I get in my bed at bedtime,
It's as crowded as can be.
    I need my sheep to help me to sleep,
    My armadillo is under the pillow,
    I've got to have Ted right here, by my head,
    I'm into the habit of cuddling rabbit,
    I sleep with a doll, I sleep with a troll,
There's no room left for me, BUMP!

☆ This is a cumulative rhyme – it grows as a new toy is added in each verse.

🚀 Use pictures or real toys to help children remember the sequence as each new toy is introduced.

🚀 The children may like to extend the number of toys in the chant by making up new rhymes, e.g:
I put my green frog next to my dog; I find room for panda, her name is Amanda; I hug crocodile, he makes me smile.

rhyme
generating rhymes; sequencing

18 A plate of potatoes

Chant

A plate of potatoes, a plate of potatoes,
There's nothing as great
As a plate of potatoes!

1st solo:	Baked in foil, fried in oil,
All:	There's nothing as great
	As a plate of potatoes!

2nd solo:	Cooked in a curry, boiled in a hurry,
All:	There's nothing as great
	As a plate of potatoes!

3rd solo:	Stewed in a pot? Give me the lot!
All:	There's nothing as great
	As a plate of potatoes!

4th solo:	Mashed with cheese? Mmm, yes please!
All:	There's nothing as great
	As a plate of potatoes!

A plate of potatoes, a plate of potatoes,
There's nothing as great
As a plate of potatoes!

☆ The rhyming couplets describing different cooking methods give children experience of rhymes. The chant can be performed by all the children, with four soloists, or groups of children saying the first line of the middle four verses.

 Older children can explore the rhyming words: *foil, oil; curry, hurry; pot, lot; cheese, please.* Notice the same spelling patterns (rime) in the first three and the different spellings in the last verse.

 Ask the children to make more recipe chants using the same structure as this with one rhyming couplet for each verse.

A plate of spaghetti ...
Topped with sauce, tomato, of course ...

Beans on toast ...
Heated through, they're good for you ...

rhyme
generating rhymes

19 Little red jeep

Chant

Let's go for a drive in the little red jeep,
Beep, beep! Beep-beep-beep!
Drive up the mountain, tall and steep,
Beep, beep! Beep-beep-beep!

Over the mountain, down we go,
Beep, beep! Beep-beep-beep!
On with the brake now, nice and slow,
Beep, beep! Beep-beep-beep!

Into the town with lots of shops,
Beep, beep! Beep-beep-beep!
Driving slow, with starts and stops,
Beep, beep! Beep-beep-beep!

The stars are out, it's time to sleep,
Beep, beep! Beep-beep-beep!
Say goodnight to the little red jeep,
Beep, beep! Beep-beep-beep!

☆ Ask the children to chant the *beep* pattern after you say the first and third lines of each verse. Then teach them the whole chant.

🚀 Ask the children to make up more verses describing the little red jeep's journey.

♫ Extend the listening skills of the children by varying the tempo. Chant each verse at a different tempo. Can the children copy the tempo with their *beep beep* response?

♪ Whisper the last verse, asking the children to match your volume.

rhyme
generating rhymes; listening skills; tempo

20 When I feel sad

Chant

When I feel sad I *hum* a song.
   Ha-ha-hum, ha-ha-hum, ha-ha-ha-ha-hum,
I *hum* a song when it all goes wrong.
   Ha-ha-hum, ha-ha-hum, ha-ha-ha-ha-hum,
I *hum* a song all through the day.
   Ha-ha-hum, ha-ha-hum, ha-ha-ha-ha-hum,
Until that sadness goes away.
   Ha-ha-hum, ha-ha-hum, ha-ha-ha-ha-hum,
   Ha-ha-hum, ha-ha-hum, ha-ha-ha-ha-hum.

When I feel sad I *dum* a song.
   Da-da-dum, da-da-dum, da-da-da-da-dum ...

When I feel sad I *fum* a song.
   Fa-fa-fum, fa-fa-fum, fa-fa-fa-fa-fum ...

☆ This chant encourages children to discriminate between sounds.

🚀 Teach the chant. Then ask the children to make up new verses, e.g. *mum: ma-ma-mum; lum: la-la-lum; glum: gla-gla-glum ...*

🚀 When the children know the chant well, play with the sound patterns by altering the speed and rhythm, then ask the children to copy accurately.

♪♪ Add percussion instruments to the sound patterns or substitute the sound words with rhythms.

🚀 Adapt the song to explore different sounds:
When I get ill, I bong my bell,
Binga-bong, binga-bong,
binga-binga-binga-bong;
I bong my bell till I get well,
Binga-bong, binga-bong,
binga-binga-binga-bong ...

exploring onset and rime through analogy
extending sound play; listening skills

21 Seaside song

Tune: Skip to my Lou

Giggling baby, *hee, hee, hee,*
Giggling baby, *hee, hee, hee,*
Giggling baby, *hee, hee, hee,*
Hee, hee, hee, hee, my darling.

Chorus: *Hee, hee, hee-hee, hee-hee,*
             Hee, hee, hee-hee, hee-hee,
             Hee, hee, hee-hee, hee-hee,
             Hee, hee, hee, hee, my darling.

Buzzing insect, *bee, bee, bee ...*

Chorus: *Bee, bee, bee-bee, bee-bee ...*

Waves on the seashore, *shee, shee, shee ...*

Chorus: *Shee, shee, shee-shee, shee-shee ...*

Throwing beach-balls, *whee, whee, whee ...*

Chorus: *Whee, whee, whee-whee, whee-whee ...*

Here at the seaside, one, two, three ...
Hee, bee, shee, whee, my darling.

Chorus: *Hee, bee, hee-bee, shee-whee ...*
             Hee, bee, shee, whee, my darling.

☆ Notice the onset (*h, b, sh, wh*) and rime (*-ee, -oo*) in *Seaside song* and *Spooky song* (opposite). Draw the children's attention to their written forms. Make pictures to illustrate each version of the song, encouraging the children to add the sound words.

🚀 Make up new verses of the song, choosing different scenes and sound patterns.

🎵 Add a different instrumental sound to each *-ee* or *-oo* word.

F♯ F♯ D D F♯ F♯ A   **exploring onset and rime through analogy**
Gig-gling ba-by, *hee, hee, hee*   -ee

22 Spooky song

Tune: *Skip to my Lou*

Owl at midnight, *hoo, hoo, hoo,*
Owl at midnight, *hoo, hoo, hoo,*
Owl at midnight, *hoo, hoo, hoo,*
Hoo, hoo, hoo, hoo, so spooky.

Chorus: *Hoo, hoo, hoo-hoo, hoo-hoo,*
Hoo, hoo, hoo-hoo, hoo-hoo,
Hoo, hoo, hoo-hoo, hoo-hoo,
Hoo, hoo, hoo, hoo, so spooky.

Hide in the darkness, *boo, boo, boo ...*

Chorus: *Boo, boo, boo-boo, boo-boo ...*

Bats in the belfry, *shoo, shoo, shoo ...*

Chorus: *Shoo, shoo, shoo-shoo, shoo-shoo ...*

Whistling wild wind, *whoo, whoo, whoo ...*

Chorus: *Whoo, whoo, whoo-whoo, whoo-whoo ...*

Don't leave me here, I'll come too ...
Hoo, boo, shoo, whoo, so spooky.

Chorus: *Hoo, boo, hoo-boo, shoo-whoo ...*
Hoo, boo, shoo, whoo, so spooky.

photocopiable pictures

F♯ F♯ D D F♯ F♯ A
Owl at mid-night, *hoo, hoo, hoo*

exploring onset and rime through analogy
-oo

23 The hungry rabbit

Tune: There was a princess long ago

I saw a hungry rabbit *hop*,
    Hop, hop, hop; hop, hop, hop;
I saw a hungry rabbit *hop*,
    Hop, hop, hop.

He climbed a hill right to the *top*,
    Top, top, top; top, top, top;
He climbed a hill right to the *top*,
    Top, top, top.

He spied a farmer's juicy *crop*,
    Crop, crop, crop ...

Ripe carrots he began to *chop*,
    Chop, chop, chop ...

  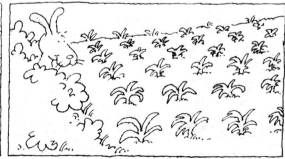 

23 The hungry rabbit – photocopiable pictures

The angry farmer shouted, "Stop!
  Stop, stop, stop ..."

He aimed his gun and it went *pop*,
  Pop, pop, pop ...

The rabbit let the carrots *drop*,
  Drop, drop, drop ...

As he escaped his ears went *flop*,
  Flop, flop, flop ...

"Next time I'll buy lunch in a *shop*,
  Shop, shop, shop ..."

⭐ This is a story song which features onset and rime, and reinforces sequencing. Ask the children to predict some of the *-op* words at the end of each new line.

🚀 Play a picture game. Make a series of nine pictures illustrating the story with one *-op* word in each frame. Make cards with the pictures and ask the children to sequence them.

🚀 Play a word game. Make a set of nine cards on which each of the nine words is written. Can the children sequence these as the song is sung, or match them to a strip of pictures?

🎵 Play a different instrument sound with each *-op* word.

A B A G E D F♯ F♯
I saw a hun-gry rab-bit *hop*

exploring onset and rime through analogy
-op; sequencing

24 Old MacGregor's holiday

Tune: Old MacDonald had a farm

Old MacGregor's at the beach, ee i ee i o.
She's throwing pebbles in the sea, ee i ee i o.
   With a *blip-blop* here and a *blip-blop* there,
    Here a *blip*, there a *blop*, everywhere a *blip-blop*,
Old MacGregor's at the beach, ee i ee i o.

Old MacGregor's at the beach, ee i ee i o.
She's going on a donkey ride, ee i ee i o.
   With a *clip-clop* here and a *clip-clop* there,
    Here a *clip*, there a *clop*, everywhere a *clip-clop*,
Old MacGregor's at the beach, ee i ee i o.

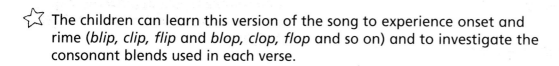

... She's watching fish in rocky pools ... *flip-flop* ...

... She's hoping that it doesn't rain ... *plip-plop* ...

... She's spreading cream so she won't burn ... *slip-slop* ...

☆ The children can learn this version of the song to experience onset and rime (*blip, clip, flip* and *blop, clop, flop* and so on) and to investigate the consonant blends used in each verse.

G G G D E E D
Old Mac-Gre-gor's at the beach

exploring onset and rime through analogy
blends featuring l; -ip, -op endings

25 The bat and cat

Tune: The farmer's in the den

Short vowels and CVC words:

The *bat* and *cat* are *fat*,
The *bat* and *cat* are *fat*,
A e i o u,
The *bat* and *cat* are *fat*.

The *pet* I *met* got *wet* ...

The *pin* and *bin* are *tin* ...

The *pot* is *not* so *hot* ...

The *bug* will *tug* the *rug* ...

Long vowels:

He *wakes* and *takes* the *cakes*,
He *wakes* and *takes* the *cakes*,
A e i o u,
He *wakes* and *takes* the *cakes*.

☆ This simple song develops an awareness of onset and rime. In each verse, the onset changes and the rime stays the same. Sing each verse at a tempo which is comfortable for the children. For the short vowel version, sing *a e i o u with* short vowel sounds, and tap fists together on each letter to accentuate the short sounds.

🚀 Encourage the children to make up more verses of their own, e.g. *A sad lad feeling bad ... A red ted in a bed ... The drum and plum are glum ...*

🚀 Sing the long vowel version of the song, with long vowel sounds on *a e i o u,* sliding palms on each letter to accentuate the long sounds. Make up more verses using long vowel sounds, e.g. *We eat meat for a treat ... The mice and rice are nice ... I hold the gold she sold ... The tube is not a cube ...*

🚀 Develop the onset and rime to include more complex spelling patterns, e.g. *See loads of toads on roads ... A flight at night is right ...*

E E G G A A G
The *bat* and *cat* are *fat*

exploring onset and rime through analogy
CVC words; short and long vowels

26 Animals' alphabet rap

Rap

Big letters, little letters, alphabet rap,
From A to Z we'll travel without looking at the map!

Big A, little a, bouncing B,
The cat's in the cupboard and she can't see me!

Big D, little d, energetic E,
The frog and the fish are feeding with the flea.

Big G, little g, H, I, J,
The kangaroo and kitten are keen to kick all day.

Big L, little l, M, N, O,
The parrot's pecking pawpaws, spitting all the pips below.

Big Q, little q, R, S, T,
The unicorn's unhappy (he's unreal, you see).

Big V, little v, W X Y,
The zappy zebra zigzags to get her stripes dry.

Big letters, little letters, alphabet beat,
All twenty-six from A to Z and no-one had to cheat!

☆ This alphabet rap reinforces the alphabet and also gives the sounds of some of the letters. Introduce it two lines at a time, asking the children to copy you.

🚀 If you wish, you can change the words *Big letters, little letters* in the first and second last lines of the rap to *Capitals, lower case.*

🚀 Divide the children into two groups to perform alternate lines of the rap.

🚀 Choose children to hold up the letters *C, F, K, P, U* and *Z* at the appropriate points in the rap. If you wish, the children can say these letters after each alternate line:
*Big A, little a, bouncing B, **C!***
The cat's in the cupboard and she can't see me ...

♫ Add body percussion or an instrumental accompaniment.

alphabet
alliteration; sequencing

27 Alphabet's tea

Tune: Bobby Shaftoe

A B C D E F G,
All the letters came to tea,
H I J K L M N,
The food was quite delicious.
O P Q R S T U,
V and W, they came too,
X and Y ate all the pie,
And Z washed up the dishes.

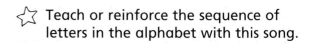 Teach or reinforce the sequence of letters in the alphabet with this song.

Using an enlarged photocopy of the alphabet rainbow here, ask a child to point to each letter at the appropriate place in the song. (By presenting the alphabet in a rainbow shape, all the letters are contained within the visual field.)

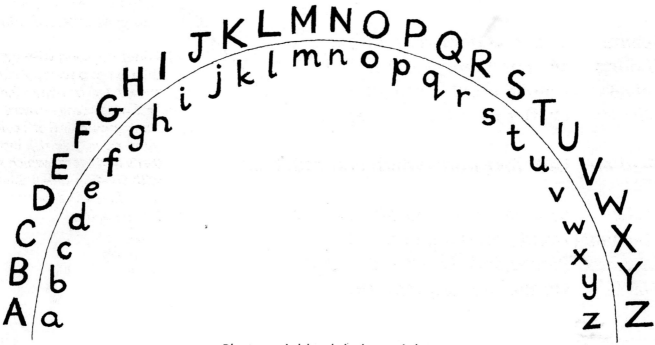

Photocopiable alphabet rainbow

F F F B♭ A C' A F
A B C D E F G

**alphabet
sequence**

28 What shall we do?

*Tune: **What shall we do with the drunken sailor?***

What shall we do with the letter *d*?
What shall we do with the letter *d*?
What shall we do with the letter *d*
On this Monday morning?

Teacher: Let's find words which start with *d*,
All: Let's find words which start with *d*,
                    Let's find words which start with *d*
                    On this Monday morning.

Samira: *Desk* and *door* start with *d*,
Thomas: *Ding* and *dong* start with *d*,
Belinda: *Do* and *don't* start with *d*
All: On this Monday morning.

Teacher: Let's find words which end with *d* ...

Lucia: *Send* and *find* end with *d*,
Stephen: *Hand* and *stand* end with *d*,
Edward: *Played* and *stayed* end with *d*
All: On this Monday morning.

☆ Choose a letter and ask the children to contribute words to make up new verses for the song. Ask individual children to sing a pair of words beginning (or ending) with the chosen letter.

🚀 Extend the vocabulary of younger children by inventing new verses, e.g. *Let's find names of farmyard animals ... (or types of transport, different colours).*

🚀 Adapt the song with older children to develop their knowledge of rhyme (*Let's find words which rhyme with Sam*), grammar (*Let's collect some 'doing' words*), letters (*Let's find words which start with vowels*), or syllables (*Let's find words which have two syllables*).

A   A   A   A   A   A   A   D FA
What shall we do with the let-ter *d*?

**letters
finding letters in words**

29 Action letters

Tune: A-ram-sam-sam

Africa (action letters: s m l)

A slinky snake, a slinky snake,

A million monkeys and a slinky snake,

A lion, a lion,

A million monkeys and a slinky snake.

Arctic (action letters: e w i)

An eskimo, an eskimo,
A whiskery walrus and an eskimo,
An igloo, an igloo,
A whiskery walrus and an eskimo.

Park (action letters: p r s)

A paddling pool, a paddling pool,
A roundabout and a paddling pool,
A seesaw, a seesaw,
A roundabout and a paddling pool.

C F F F C F F F
A slin-ky snake, a slin-ky snake

☆ As the children sing, they draw each letter shape in the air.

🚀 Think of new verses. Here are two examples:
Toys (b t j)
A bicycle, a bicycle,
Tyrannosaurus rex and a bicycle,
A jigsaw, a jigsaw ...
Pets (c h g)
A cuddly cat, a cuddly cat,
A hairy hamster and a cuddly cat,
A gerbil, a gerbil ...

🎵 Sing a verse as a round in two or three groups, with actions.

letters
writing letter shapes

30 Teatime treats

Tune: Polly put the kettle on

Polly puts the pizza in,
Polly puts the pizza in,
Polly puts the pizza in,
We'll all have tea.
  Sukey sizzles sausages,
  Sukey sizzles sausages,
  Sukey sizzles sausages,
  We'll all have tea.

The children can use their own names, and find a food which begins with the same letter or sound to make more verses, e.g. *Ben bites biscuits bit by bit; Carli crunched a carrot cake.*

Notice names which begin with short vowel sounds, e.g. *Anna asks for apple pie,* and those which have long vowel sounds, e.g. *Amy aims for apricots.*

Invent your own verses, working through the alphabet.

C' D' C' B♭ A F F
Pol-ly puts the piz-za in

**letters
alliteration**

31 'Magic e'

Tune: Girls and boys come out to play

'Magic e', oh, 'magic e',
Casting spells so easily,
At to *ate* and *mat* to *mate*,
Wizardry with 'magic e'.

Use this song to explore words which change, e.g:
hat to *hate* and *fat* to *fate*;
tap to *tape* and *cap* to *cape*;
win to *wine* and *din* to *dine*;
pip to *pipe* and *strip* to *stripe*;
cod to *code* and *rod* to *rode*;
cub to *cube* and *tub* to *tube*.

A F♯ G E A F♯ D
'Ma-gic e', oh, 'ma-gic e'

**letters
'magic e'; spelling**

32 Bingo lingo

Bingo – adapted

There was a farmer with a dog and *Bingo* was his name-o,
    B – I – N-G-O,
    B – I – N-G-O,
    B – I – N-G-O,
And *Bingo* was his name-o.

There was a goldfish with a son and *Fingo* was his name-o,
    F – I – N-G-O,
    F – I – N-G-O,
    F – I – N-G-O,
And *Fingo* was his name-o.

There was a princess with a dad and *Kingo* was his name-o,
    K – I – N-G-O ...

There was a penguin with a chick and *Pingo* was her name-o ...

There was a pop-star with some drums and *Ringo* was his name-o ...

There was a schoolgirl with a bike and *Tingo* was its name-o ...

D   G G D   D   E   E D   D   G G A A   B   G
There was a far-mer with a dog and *Bin-go* was his name-o

There was a robot with a friend and *Zingo* was her name-o ...

Now sing these names along with me
And we'll speak *Bingo Lingo*,
    B – I – N-G-O,
    L – I – N-G-O,
    Bingo, Fingo, Kingo, Pingo,
Ringo, Tingo, Zingo.

 Teach the first verse of the song. Then sing the first line of each of the following verses, omitting the first letter when spelling each name: * – I – N-G-O. Can the children supply the initial consonant and sing it at the appropriate time? (They may need to listen first then add the new letter when the verse is sung a second time.)

 Break down the words into onset and rime: *B–ingo; F–ingo* ...

 Sing each section spelling the name in two groups: group 1: *B*, group 2: – *I* – N-G-O.

 Make a set of letter cards with the capital letters *B F K P R T Z*. Can the children choose the matching letter card as each verse is sung?

 Find other consonants (e.g. *S W D*), and blends (e.g. *Br Cl Fl St Sl Sw Str*) to make more verses, e.g. *There was a clown who had a hat and Jingo was his name-o* ... *There was a wasp who liked to hum and Stingo was her name-o* ...

 Change the short vowel sound in each verse, e.g. *Bengo, Fengo ... Bango, Fango ... Bongo, Fongo* ...

 Change the final vowel sound, e.g. *Binga, Finga ... Bingy (y as -ee), Fingy* ...

letters
identifying initial phonemes; spelling

33 Baby's bed

Tune: Goosey, goosey gander

Make a *bed* for baby,
First you need a 'b',
'e' in the middle,
Finish with a 'd'.

Make a *cat* called Curly,
First you need a 'c',
'a' in the middle,
Finish with a 't'.

Make a *dog* called Dozy,
First you need a 'd',
'o' in the middle,
Finish with a 'g'.

Baby's in her *bed* now,
Cat curls on the floor,
As darkness falls, *dog*
Dozes by the door.

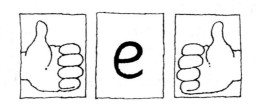

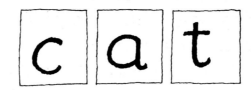

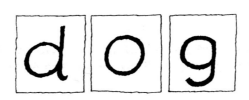

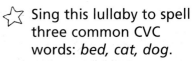 Sing this lullaby to spell three common CVC words: *bed, cat, dog.*

Show the children how to shape their left fist into a *b* and right fist into a *d*, then place together to make the bed in verse one – a useful reminder when writing these two letters which are often confused.

On three cards, write the letters *b, e* and *d*. Ask the children to order the cards as they sing verse one. Repeat this activity with *cat* and *dog*.

Give pairs or individual children all nine letter cards to make each word while singing the song.

photocopiable cards

C D C E G G
Make a bed for ba-by

letters
reading and spelling common CVC words

34 The wishing well

Tune: Greensleeves

The wishing well is on the hill,
The walls are deep, the waters chill,
The stories tell that it casts a spell,
And makes all of your wishes come true.

Chorus: Drink, traveller, drink your fill,
At the wishing well on the lonely hill.
Drink, traveller, drink your fill,
And may all of your wishes come true.

☆ After singing the song, ask the children to find all the *-ll* words. Say the words of the song together line by line, writing the *-ll* words down for the children to see.

🚀 Sort the words into three groups: *-all*, *-ell* and *-ill* endings. Stress that while e and i remain short, *a* yawns when followed by *-ll* (one exception is *shall*).

🚀 Ask the children to make new *-ll* ending words, using the onsets which appear in this song, e.g. *spell, spill; fill, fall, fell; hill, hall, hell.*

E G A BC♯ B A F♯ D
The wish-ing well is on the hill

word endings
–ll

35 Quick, duck, quack

Tune: Heads, shoulders, knees and toes

Quick! Quick, duck, quick, duck, quack,
Quick, duck, quack!
Foxy's coming down the track,
With a sack,
Your friends and you will make a lovely snack.
Quick! Quick, duck, quick, duck, quack,
Quick, duck, quack!

☆ This tongue-twister features the -ck ending. Sing the song at a
slow tempo until the children can articulate the words clearly.
Once they have become confident at singing this, they will enjoy
trying to get the words right at a faster tempo.

G	A	G	F♯	G	E
Quick! Quick, duck, quick, duck, quack					

word endings

–ck

36 Huff puff

Tune: The hokey cokey

You do a huff puff here!
A huff puff there!
Huff puff, huff puff,
Little pigs, beware!
I'm a gruff and greedy wolfie,
And I'm ready for my tea,
Here we go, one, two, three!

Chorus: Ooooh, huffy, puffy, puffy!
Ooooh, watch me do my stuffy,
How dare you call me scruffy,
I'll blow your house down, just you see!

☆ Teach the children this wolf's song from the story of the three pigs, to focus on -*ff* word endings. Collect together all the -*ff* words in this song and ask the children what they notice about them. (They are all -*uff* endings.)

🚀 Point out to older children the use of the letter -*y* at the end of *huffy, puffy, scruffy* and *stuffy*.

D E D G G
You do a huff puff here!

word endings
–ff

37 Party time

Tune: Hickory dickory dock

Jess threw a jelly at Tess!
Bess made a mess on her dress!
Joss got cross, and
Russ made a fuss,
The party was not a success!

> ☆ Find the song words ending *-ss*.
> Group them into *-ess*, *-oss* and *-uss*
> endings. Think of more words for
> each group, e.g. *chess, less, boss, loss*.
> (Discuss and explore suggestions of
> words with the same sound, but
> different spellings, e.g. *yes, bus*.)

E		F	G	G	A	B	C'

Jess threw a jel-ly at Tess

word endings

–ss

38 Sing-song

Tune: My old man's a dustman

Sing, sing, sing a sing-song,
A sing-a sing-song sang,
Sung, sung, sung a sing-song,
A sung-a sing-song sang.

Bing, bing, bing a bing-bong ...

Ding, ding, ding a ding-dong ...

> ☆ The onset of the words in this
> tongue-twister changes in each verse
> while each of the rimes (*-ing*, *-ang*,
> *-ong*, *-ung*) remain the same.

> 🚀 When the children know verse one
> well, introduce the other verses and
> ask them to find more onsets to
> make real and nonsense words, e.g.
> *ping, ting, wing, ching, swing, thing,
> pling ... pong, tong, wong, chong ...*

F#		F#		F#	F#	F#		F#

Sing, sing, sing a sing-song

word endings

–ng

39 Yes, no

Tune: She'll be coming round the mountain

Leader:	1st group:	2nd group:
Do you like to eat bananas?	Yes, I do.	No, I don't.
Do you like to eat bananas?	Yes, I do.	No, I don't.
Do you like to eat bananas,		
Like to eat bananas,		
Like to eat bananas?	Yes, I do.	No, I don't.
Can you swim one hundred metres?	Yes, I can.	No, I can't ...
Are you sitting on a pumpkin?	Yes, I am.	No, I'm not ...
Have you ever been to Norway?	Yes, I have.	No, I haven't ...
Will you be at school tomorrow?	Yes, I will.	No, I won't ...

 This song introduces the correct forms of answers to common forms of questions. Introduce one question at a time until the children are familiar and confident with the answers. They may all sing one answer together, *yes, I do*, or they can divide into groups to sing *Yes, I do,* or *No, I don't,* according to choice.

 Ask the children to invent more questions of their own and encourage them to sing them to the class, e.g. *Can you keep your bedroom tidy? Have you ever swum the Channel?*

 Working in pairs, children can take it in turns to ask questions and to reply to them.

C D F F F F D C A, C F
Do you like to eat ba-na-nas? *Yes, I do.*

grammar
questions and answers

40 What's she doing?

Tune: London's burning

Solo:
What's she doing?
That's the question.
Can you guess?
She is reading.

What's he doing?
... He is cooking.

... She is sawing ...

... He is singing ...

... She is laughing ...

All (echo):
What's she doing?
That's the question.
Can you guess?
She is reading.

What's he doing ...
He is cooking.

☆ For this song, one child mimes an action without telling the other children what it is. Another child leads the song and the rest sing the echo. The child who is leading sings the first three lines of the song, then guesses what the mime is to complete the song. Some mimes have been suggested above; the children can make up more of their own.

🚀 Point out to older children the use of the question and answer format of the song. Can they say where to put the question marks?

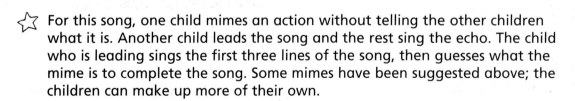

C   C   F   F   C   C   F   F
What's she do-ing? What's she do-ing?

grammar
questions and answers; verbs

41 This old lady

This old man (adapted)

Number one, number one,
Number one is just for fun.
    With a knick knack paddy whack,
    Been to see the Dome,
This old lady's *jumping* home.

Number two, number two,
Number two has work to do.
    With a knick knack paddy whack,
    Been to see the Dome,
This old lady's *swimming* home.

... Number three grows like a tree ...
... This old lady's *running* home.

... Number four feels sad and sore ...
... This old lady's *sliding* home.

... Number five says 'Snakes alive' ...
... This old lady's *cycling* home.

☆ Begin by chanting this simple fingerplay. Start by touching your thumb, then your forefinger and so on:
    Number one – just for fun
    Number two – work to do
    Number three – like a tree
    Number four – sad and sore
    Number five – snakes alive!
Then sing the song.

 Sing the song again and ask the children for more 'doing' words to get the lady home. Here are some suggestions: *creeping, skating, stamping, cycling, wobbling, riding, walking.* Discuss all the children's suggestions.

 Play a sound on a musical instrument during the last line of each verse. Choose a sound which matches the movement, e.g. *jumping* – tap wood block; *sliding* – slide a beater over the bars of a xylophone.

 Older children can begin to look at spelling rules for adding the suffix *-ing*.

A F♯ A   A F♯ A
Num-ber one, num-ber one

grammar
verbs; number sequence

42 My hat

My hat, it has three corners (adapted)

My hat, it is too *floppy*,
Too *floppy* is my hat,
Because it is too *floppy*,
I will not wear my hat!

My hat, it is too *spotty*,
Too *spotty* is my hat,
Because it is too *spotty*,
I will not wear my hat!

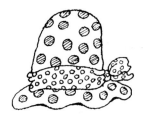

My hat, it is too *stripy*,
Too *stripy* is my hat,
Because it is too *stripy*,
I will not wear my hat!

My hat, it is too *fluffy*,
Too *fluffy* is my hat,
Because it is too *fluffy*,
I will not wear my hat!

☆ Sing the song. Then ask the children to find more adjectives to explain why they might not like their imaginary hat, e.g. *woolly, itchy, dirty, muddy, sticky, bobbly, small, big, silly, pretty*. Collect these together and discuss them. Use the children's suggestions to make up new verses for the song.

🚀 The children can design and draw, or paint the hat they have described. Make a hat shop frieze by placing all the designs on shelves, then label them with their descriptions.

♪ For each verse, choose an instrumental sound to play whenever the adjective is sung.

G C' G G F E F D
My hat, it is too flop-py

grammar
adjectives

43 Opposites

Tune: We three Kings of Orient are

Let's all play the opposites game,
Opposites are never the same.
    I say, "Yes,"
    You say, "No,"
Let's all play the game again.

Let's all play the opposites game,
Opposites are never the same.
    I say, "Day,"
    You say, "Night,"
Let's all play the game again.

    ... I say, "Up,"
    You say, "Down," ...

Let's all play the opposites game,
Opposites are never the same.
    I say, "Hot,"
    You say, "Cold,"
Now we've played the opposites game.

☆ Teach the first two verses to the children. Use the extra verses to ask them to predict the opposite.

🚀 Make more opposite verses. Here are some suggestions:
in, out; near, far; high, low; long, short; fast, slow; happy, sad; fat, thin; young, old; wet, dry; first, last.

🚀 Invite individual children to sing the opposite words: *If I say "push," then Daniel says "pull,"* ...

🚀 Change the verb, e.g. *I shout, cry, yell, whisper, croak, sing* ...

🚀 Show older children the use of speech marks in each verse. Can they write another verse, correctly placing the speech marks?

B A G E F♯ G F♯ E
Let's all play the op-po-sites game

grammar
antonyms

44 What did we read?

Tune: Here we go round the mulberry bush

Teacher:
What did we read at school today,
School today, school today?
What did we read at school today?
Remember, then we'll sing the answer.

(Meredith: *We read a story.)*

All:
We read a story at school today,
School today, school today.
We read a story at school today,
We'll read again tomorrow.

(Eliot: *We read our names.)*

All:
We read our names at school today ...

☆ Sing this song at the end of a literacy session or at the end of the school day to remind children of all the reading activities they have been involved with.

🚀 Here are other suggestions of what the children might have read:
some sounds, a poem, a letter, some labels, a big book, letter 'd' words, lots of 'sh' words, a recipe, instructions ...

🚀 Adapt the song as follows:
Teacher: *What will you read at school today ... Oh, Ali, please tell me your answer.*
Ali: *I'll read my name at school today ... I'll read again tomorrow.*

🚀 You may wish to sing *What did we write?* when this is appropriate.

F   F   F   F   A   C'   A   F
What did we read at school to-day

reviewing

Song melodies

1   Hello around the world – *If you're happy and you know it*

Solo: When you want to say *hel - lo* a - round the world, **All:** *Hel - lo!* **Solo:** When you want to say *hel - lo* a - round the world, **All:** *Hel - lo!* **Solo:** When you want to say *hel - lo,* Sing this song and you will know How to greet your friends from all a - round the world. **All:** *Hel - lo!*

3   Some names – *Pease pudding hot*

Some names are short, Some names are long. Please tell us your name Af - ter this song.

4   Old MacGregor had a zoo – *Old MacDonald had a farm (adapted)*
24   Old MacGregor's holiday

Old Mac-Gre-gor had a zoo, ee i ee i o. And in that zoo she had some *snakes*,
Old Mac-Gre-gor's at the beach, ee i ee i o. She's throw-ing peb-bles in the sea,

ee i ee i o. With a *ssss ssss* here and a *ssss ssss* there, Here a *ssss*, there a *ssss*,
ee i ee i o. With a *blip-blop* here and a *blip-blop* there, Here a *blip*, there a *blop*,

eve-ry-where a *ssss ssss*, Old Mac-Gre-gor had a zoo, ee i ee i o.
eve-ry-where a *blip-blop*, Old Mac-Gre-gor's at the beach, ee i ee i o.

6   Chatterbox – *Pat-a-cake*

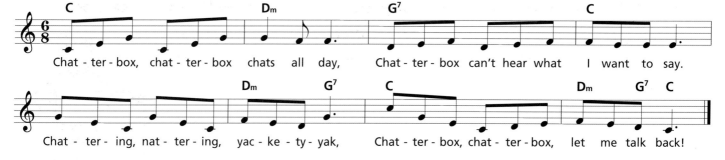

Chat-ter-box, chat-ter-box chats all day, Chat-ter-box can't hear what I want to say.

Chat-ter-ing, nat-ter-ing, yac-ke-ty-yak, Chat-ter-box, chat-ter-box, let me talk back!

7   My machine – *The wheels on the bus*

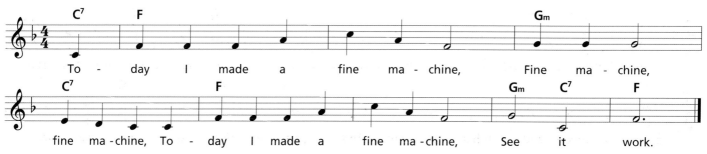

To - day I made a fine ma-chine, Fine ma-chine,

fine ma-chine, To - day I made a fine ma-chine, See it work.

10   Yoyo – *Oranges and lemons*

Once I had a yo - yo, But my yo - yo would - n't go go. My friend Flo said,

"No no! That is not the way to yo - yo. You roll it to the top top, And __

then you let it drop drop. When it climbs the string, You __ don't do a

thing. Then give a lit - tle flick flick, Now you've near - ly learnt the

trick trick." But when I tried to yo - yo, It __ still would - n't go go.

11   Grandma and the flea – *A sailor went to sea*

My Grand - ma found a flea, flea, flea, A - swim - ming in her tea, tea, tea. She

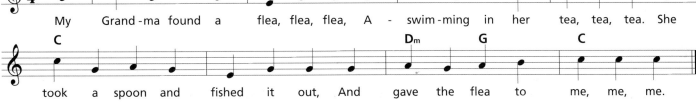

took a spoon and fished it out, And gave the flea to me, me, me.

12   Captain of the aeroplane – *John Brown's body*

I'm cap-tain of the ae-ro-plane and this is my sa-lute, I've got
shi-ny, sil-ver but-tons on my spe-cial cap-tain's suit. I climb in-to my
cock-pit and I strap my-self in tight, And we're off! En-joy the flight!_____
Can ____ you hear the en-gines roar-ing? Soon ___ we'll all be up and soar-ing,
In ____ the sky we'll go ex-plor-ing In-side my ae-ro-plane. ____

15   Hey, little playmate (1st version) – *Hush little baby (adapted)*
16   Hey, little playmate (2nd version)

Hey, lit-tle play-mate, don't you cry, I'm going to sing you a lul-la-by.
Hey, lit-tle play-mate, don't say a thing, I'm going to buy you a piece of *string.*

repeat as necessary

If that lul-la-by sounds too loud, I'm going to buy you a lit-tle cloud.
If that piece of string's too thick, I'm going to buy you a ba-by *chick.*

21   Seaside song – *Skip to my Lou*

22   Spooky song

Gig -gling ba - by,   hee, hee, hee,   Gig -gling ba - by,   hee, hee, hee,   Gig -gling ba - by,
Owl at mid - night,   hoo, hoo, hoo,   Owl at mid- night,   hoo, hoo, hoo,   Owl at mid- night,

hee, hee, hee,   Hee, hee, hee, hee, my   dar - ling.   Hee, hee,   hee-hee, hee- hee,   Hee, hee,
hoo, hoo, hoo,   Hoo, hoo, hoo, hoo, so   spook- y.   Hoo, hoo,   hoo-hoo, hoo- hoo,   Hoo, hoo,

hee - hee, hee - hee,   Hee, hee,   hee - hee, hee -hee,   Hee, hee, hee, hee, my   dar - ling.
hoo - hoo, hoo -hoo,   Hoo, hoo,   hoo - hoo, hoo- hoo,   Hoo, hoo, hoo, hoo, so   spook- y.

23   The hungry rabbit – *There was a princess long ago*

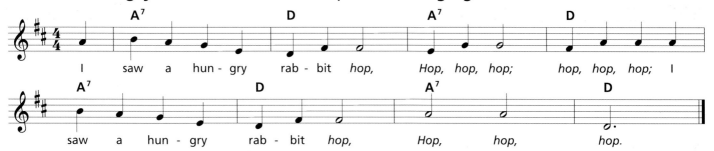

I   saw   a   hun - gry   rab - bit   hop,   Hop, hop, hop;   hop, hop, hop;   I

saw   a   hun - gry   rab - bit   hop,   Hop,   hop,   hop.

24   Old MacGregor's holiday – see 4

25   The bat and cat – *The farmer's in the den*

The   *bat*   and   *cat*   are   *fat,*   The   *bat*   and   *cat*   are   *fat,*

A   e   i   o   u,   The   *bat*   and   *cat*   are   *fat.*

27 Alphabet's tea – *Bobby Shaftoe*

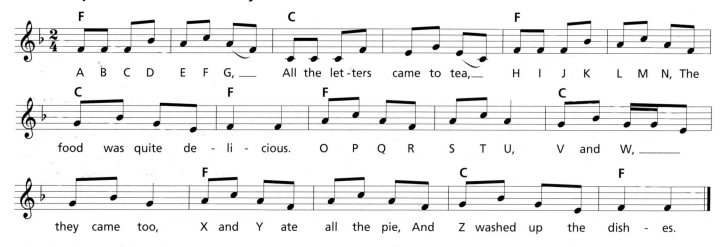

A B C D E F G, __ All the let-ters came to tea, __ H I J K L M N, The

food was quite de-li-cious. O P Q R S T U, V and W, _____

they came too, X and Y ate all the pie, And Z washed up the dish-es.

28 What shall we do? – *What shall we do with the drunken sailor?*

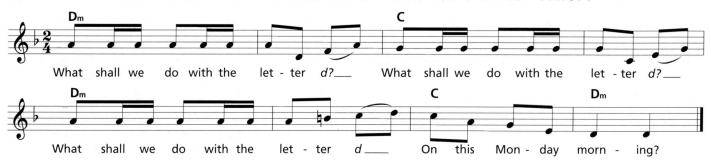

What shall we do with the let-ter d? __ What shall we do with the let-ter d? __

What shall we do with the let-ter d __ On this Mon-day morn-ing?

29 Action letters – *A-ram-sam-sam*

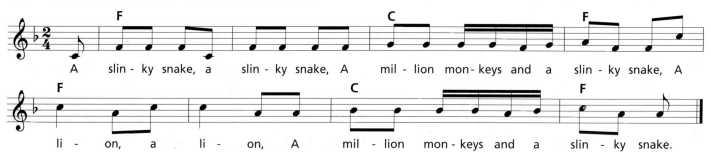

A slin-ky snake, a slin-ky snake, A mil-lion mon-keys and a slin-ky snake, A

li-on, a li-on, A mil-lion mon-keys and a slin-ky snake.

30   Teatime treats – *Polly put the kettle on*

Pol - ly puts the piz - za in,   Pol - ly puts the piz - za in,

Pol - ly puts the piz - za in, We'll all have tea.   Su - key siz - zles sau - sa - ges,

Su - key siz - zles sau - sa - ges,   Su - key siz - zles sau - sa - ges, We'll all have tea.

31   'Magic e' – *Girls and boys come out to play*

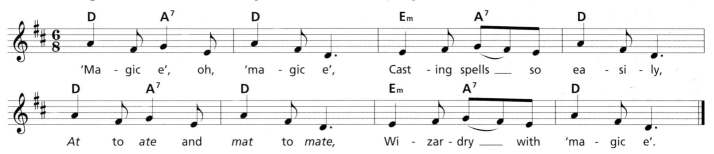

'Ma - gic e', oh, 'ma - gic e',   Cast - ing spells ___ so ea - si - ly,

At to *ate* and *mat* to *mate,*   Wi - zar - dry ___ with 'ma - gic e'.

32   Bingo lingo – *Bingo*

There was a farm - er with a dog and *Bin - go* was his name - o,   B I N G O,

B I N G O,   B I N G O, And *Bin - go* was his name - o.

33   Baby's bed – *Goosey, goosey gander*

Make a bed for ba - by, First you need a 'b', 'e' in the mid - dle, Fi - nish with a 'd'.

34   The wishing well – *Greensleeves*

The wish - ing well___ is on the hill, ___ The walls are deep, ___ the wa - ters chill, The

sto - ries tell that it casts a spell, And makes all of your wi - shes come true. _____

Drink, tra - vel - ler, drink your fill, At the wish - ing well on the lone - ly hill.

Drink, tra - vel - ler, drink your fill, And may all of your wi - shes come true. _____

35   Quick, duck, quack – *Heads, shoulders, knees and toes*

Quick!   Quick, duck, quick, duck, quack, Quick, duck, quack!

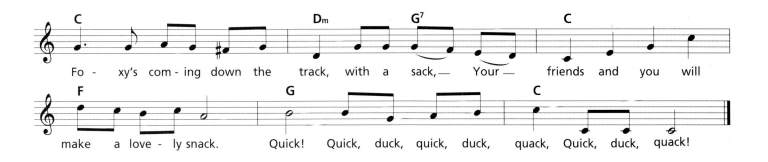

Foxy's coming down the track, with a sack,— Your — friends and you will make a love-ly snack. Quick! Quick, duck, quick, duck, quack, Quick, duck, quack!

36   Huff, puff – *The hokey cokey*

You do a huff puff here! A huff puff there! Huff puff, huff puff, Lit-tle pigs, be-ware! I'm a gruff and greed-y wol-fie, And I'm rea-dy for my tea, Here we go, one, two, three!

Ooooh, huf-fy, puf-fy, puf-fy! — Ooooh, watch me do my stuf-fy, —

How dare you call me scruf-fy, — I'll blow your house down, just you see!

37   Party time – *Hickory dickory dock*

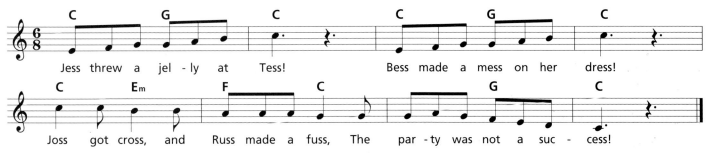

Jess threw a jel-ly at Tess! Bess made a mess on her dress!

Joss got cross, and Russ made a fuss, The par-ty was not a suc-cess!

38   Sing-song – *My old man's a dustman*

Sing, sing, sing   a sing-song, A   sing - a sing-song sang,   Sung, sung, sung a sing-song, A   sung- a sing-song sang.

39   Yes, no – *She'll be coming round the mountain*

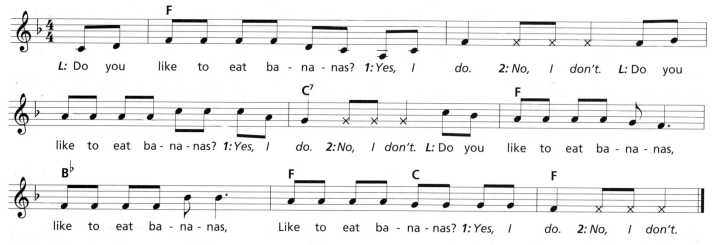

L: Do you   like   to   eat   ba - na - nas?   *1:*Yes,   I   do.   *2:*No,   I   don't.   L: Do   you

like   to   eat   ba - na - nas?   *1:*Yes,   I   do.   *2:*No,   I   don't.   L: Do you   like   to   eat   ba - na - nas,

like   to   eat   ba - na - nas,   Like   to   eat   ba - na - nas?   *1:*Yes,   I   do.   *2:*No,   I   don't.

40   What's she doing? – *London's burning*

S: What's   she   do - ing? *A:* What's   she   do - ing? *S:* That's   the   ques - tion. *A:* That's   the

ques - tion. *S:*Can   you   guess?   *A:* Can   you   guess?   *S:* She   is   read - ing. *A:* She   is   read - ing.

41   This old lady – *This old man (adapted)*

Num - ber   one,   num - ber   one,   Num - ber   one   is   just   for   fun.   With   a

knick knack pad - dy whack, Been to see the Dome, This old la - dy's *jump - ing* home.

42 **My hat** – *My hat, it has three corners (adapted)*

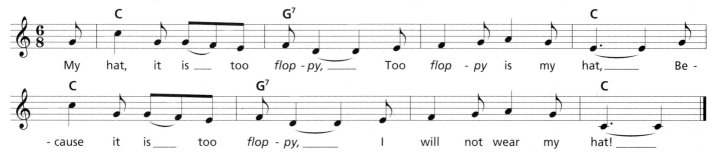

My hat, it is ___ too *flop - py,* ___ Too *flop - py* is my hat, ___ Be -

- cause it is ___ too *flop - py,* ___ I will not wear my hat! ___

43 **Opposites** – *We three Kings of Orient are*

Let's all play the op - po - sites game, Op - po - sites are ne - ver the same.

I say, "Yes," You say, "No," ___ Let's all play the game a - gain.

44 **What did we read?** – *Here we go round the mulberry bush*

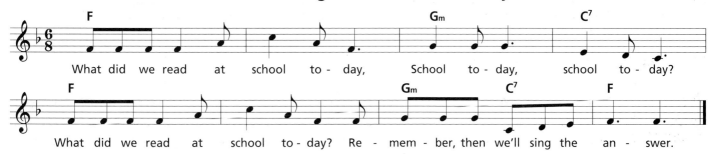

What did we read at school to - day, School to - day, school to - day?

What did we read at school to - day? Re - mem - ber, then we'll sing the an - swer.

First lines index